S0-EHX-649

My Weirdtastic School #6

Ms. Greene Is Mean!

Dan Gutman

Pictures by
Jim Paillot

HARPER

An Imprint of HarperCollinsPublishers

To all the math teachers

Special thanks to these terrific teachers for their feedback and suggestions: Harley Abrevaya, Colleen Amaral, Lisa Anne, Alison Thomes Beedy, BendanLo and July Bennett, Emily Bryant, Chantal Castille, Amanda Cleary Deal, Karen Dent, Mrs. DiLillo, Sue Ernst, Joshua Ezekiel, Tamara Fay, Krystin Feole, Basil Frankweiler, Symberly Breann Glisson, Tammy Docter Goodman, Allison Jane, Tina Koenig, Patty Kropp, Ash Lee, Wendy Bowman-Levine, Kristin Mason, Mrs. Messina, Julie Gordon Olson, Jodi Waldan Ritacco, Sarah Rogers, Amy Sandler, Amy Simon, Michelle Snyder, Megan Snover, Mrs. Tanner, Leslie Bailin Weintraub, and Mary Zdrojewski.

My Weirdtastic School #6: Ms. Greene Is Mean!
Text copyright © 2024 by Dan Gutman
Illustrations copyright © 2024 by Jim Paillot
All rights reserved. Printed in the United States of America.
No part of this book may be used or reproduced in any manner whatsoever without written permission except in the case of brief quotations embodied in critical articles and reviews. For information address HarperCollins Children's Books, a division of HarperCollins Publishers, 195 Broadway, New York, NY 10007.
www.harpercollinschildrens.com

Library of Congress Control Number: 2023948794
ISBN 978-0-06-320716-5 (pbk bdg) — ISBN 978-0-06-320717-2 (trade bdg)

Typography by Laura Mock
24 25 26 27 28   PC/CWR   10 9 8 7 6 5 4 3 2 1

First Edition

Contents

Math Is Everywhere!

My name is A.J., and I know what you're thinking. You're thinking about sporks. Because that's what I'm thinking about. A spork is a tool that is a spoon and a fork all in one. I heard you can also get a knife and a fork all in one. It's called a knork. I think somebody should invent a combination fork, spoon, and knife. They could call it a knoof.

The point is, we had just arrived in Miss Banks's class on Monday morning.

"I have an announcement to make," Miss Banks said as we put our backpacks in our cubbies and sat down. "I'm not going to teach math today."

"YAY!" everybody shouted, which is also "YAY" backward. We all high-fived each other.

"Just kidding," said Miss Banks. "We do math *every* day!"

"BOO!" everybody shouted, which is "OOB" backward. Miss Banks pulls lots of pranks.

"Time is fun when you're having flies!" she said. "Turn to page twenty-three in your math books."

Ugh. Math stinks! Why do we need to learn math if we have calculators? But we never had the chance to open our math books. You'll never believe who walked through the door at that moment.

Nobody! You can't walk through a door. Doors are made of wood. But you'll never believe who walked through the door*way*.

It was our principal, Mrs. Stoker.

"To what do I owe the pleasure of your company?" asked Miss Banks.

That's grown-up talk for "What are *you* doing here?"

"I have an important announcement," said Mrs. Stoker. "But first, do you know why six was afraid of seven?"

"Why?" we all asked.

"Because seven ate nine!" she said. "Get it?"

That's the oldest joke in the book. But

we all laughed because you should always laugh at the principal's jokes. Mrs. Stoker is a joker. When she's not our principal, she's a stand-up comedian.

"Hey," said Mrs. Stoker, "why can't a nose be twelve inches long?"

"Why?" we asked.

"Because then it would be a foot!" said Mrs. Stoker. She slapped her knee because grown-ups always slap their knee when they think something is funny. Nobody knows why.

"But seriously," said Mrs. Stoker. "Miss Banks isn't going to teach you math today."

"For real?" I asked.

"Yes, for real!"

"YAY!" we all shouted, high-fiving each other again.

"Because somebody *else* is going to teach you math today," said Mrs. Stoker.

WHAT?!

"The math scores at Ella Mentry School are way down," said Mrs. Stoker. "So I decided to bring in a math expert to help us improve our scores."

"BOO!" we all shouted, except for Andrea Young, this annoying girl with curly brown hair.

"I love math!" said Andrea.

"I love math too," said Emily, who always loves everything Andrea loves.

"Then you're *really* going to love Ms.

Greene," said Mrs. Stoker.

A lady came into the room. She was wearing a dress that had numbers all over it.

"Hi!" said Ms. Greene. "Say, how many of you hate math?"

"I do!" said Ryan, who will eat anything, even stuff that isn't food.

"I do!" said Neil, who we call the nude kid even though he wears clothes.

"Math stinks!" I said.

Mrs. Stoker told us she had to go to a meeting. Principals are always going to meetings. Nobody knows why.

"I'll stop by later to see how you're making out," she said.

Ugh, gross! I'm not going to make out with anybody.

"Why do I need to learn math?" Alexia asked after Mrs. Stoker left. "I'm not going to become a math teacher. When I grow up, I'm going to be a professional skateboarder."

"Oh, skateboarding is all *about* math!" said Ms. Greene.

"No way," said Alexia.

"What is it called when you jump up, spin around on your skateboard, and land facing the opposite direction?" asked Ms. Greene.

"That's called a one-eighty," Alexia replied. She knows all about skateboarding.

"Right," said Ms. Greene. "You spin your skateboard around a hundred eighty degrees. That's half a circle. And what's it called when you spin *all* the way around?"

"That's called a three-sixty," Alexia told her.

"Correct," said Ms. Greene. "There are three hundred sixty degrees in a circle, and one hundred eighty times two is three hundred sixty. And what's it called when you spin around *twice*?"

"That's a seven-twenty," Alexia told her.

"Very good," said Ms. Greene. "Because three hundred sixty times two equals seven hundred twenty. And if you spun around *three* times it would be a thousand-eighty. That's math! Math is everywhere!"

"I never thought of that," admitted Alexia.

"Oh, yeah?" said Michael, who never ties his shoes. "I don't like skateboarding. I like football, and when I grow up, I'm going to be a pro football player. I won't need to know math."

"Sure you will," said Ms. Greene. "Football is all about math."

"No way," said Michael.

"Let's say your team is losing twenty-one to fourteen," said Ms. Greene. "You have the ball on your own forty-yard line. How many yards do you need to move the ball to score a touchdown?"

"Sixty yards," replied Michael.

"Right," said Ms. Greene. "A football field is a hundred yards long, and a hundred minus forty equals sixty. And let's say you score a touchdown on the next play. What's the score *now*?"

"Twenty-one to twenty," replied Michael.

"Correct," said Ms. Greene. "Because

a touchdown is six points, and fourteen plus six equals twenty. So do you kick the extra point?"

"Well," said Michael, "if we kick the extra point, it will tie the game at twenty-one to twenty-one. Or, we could go for the two-point conversion to take a twenty-two to twenty-one lead."

"See?" said Ms. Greene. "That's football math!"

"I never thought of that," admitted Michael.

Neil said he likes video games, and Ms. Greene showed how video games are all about math. Emily said she likes horses, and Ms. Greene showed how horses are all about math. Every time somebody brought up a subject, Ms. Greene showed how it was all about math.*

"You see," she said, "math is *everywhere*! Any subject you can name—"

She didn't have the chance to finish her sentence because that's when the weirdest thing in the history of the world happened. But I'm not going to tell you what it was.

Okay, okay, I'll tell you. But you have to read the next chapter. So nah-nah-nah boo-boo on you!

---

*There are ten things you can always count on—your fingers.

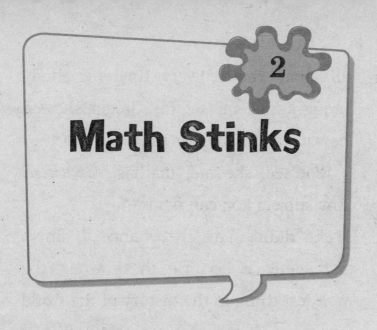

Math Stinks

The weird thing that happened was that somebody farted.

Okay, I said it. I know you're not supposed to talk about farting in a children's book. Nobody knows why. But it happened! Farting is part of life. Anyway, Ms. Greene was telling Ryan how soccer was all about math when somebody let out a loud fart.

It was the funniest thing in the history of the world. Everybody started giggling. You should always giggle when somebody farts. That's the first rule of being a kid. Farting is hilarious. Nobody knows why. I bet when some caveman blasted out the first fart, the other people in the cave started giggling.

"Who farted?" I asked.

"It wasn't me," said Ryan.

"Wasn't me," said Michael.

"Wasn't me," said Neil.

Nobody wanted to admit they farted.

"It doesn't *matter* who farted," said Ms. Greene. "Farting is all about math *too*!"

"WHAT?!" we all said.

"Did you know that the average person

farts twenty times a day?" asked Ms. Greene.

"WOW," we all said, which is also "WOW" backward.

"How many students go to Ella Mentry School?" asked Ms. Greene.

"About two hundred," replied Miss Banks.

"So if two hundred kids each fart twenty times in a day," said Ms. Greene, "how many times does the whole school fart every day?"

Everybody rushed to get out pencils and papers so they could figure out how much the school farts every day. Andrea was the first one to come up with the answer, *of course*.

"Two hundred times twenty equals four thousand," she said. Then she smiled the smile she smiles to let everybody know she knows something nobody else knows.

"Right!" said Ms. Greene. "So the kids at Ella Mentry School fart four thousand times each day."

"WOW," we all said, which is "MOM" upside down.

"Farting is all about math," said Ms. Greene. "Math is *everywhere*!"*

"And that's why math stinks," I said.

"I didn't know our school farted so much," said Ryan. "Four thousand farts!"

"And that's not even counting the teachers," said Alexia.

"Teachers never fart," insisted Miss Banks.

They do too. Everybody farts. Even teachers. And do you want to know a secret? I know who let out the fart that started the whole discussion.

It was me. *Shhhh*, don't tell anybody.

---

*Do you know what's odd? Every other number.

Ms. Greene Is Mean

We didn't see Ms. Greene for a week after that. Miss Banks told us that Ms. Greene would be coming to our class once a week, every Monday, to help us with our math skills. Sure enough, the next Monday she was back.

"Are you ready for NUMMM-BERS?"

she shouted, like a wrestling announcer.

"Yes!" shouted all the girls.

"No!" shouted all the boys.

Alexia leaned over to me when Ms. Greene took off her coat.

"I think Ms. Greene is pregnant," she whispered.

"How do you know?" I whispered back.

"She has a baby bump on her tummy," Alexia whispered.

"I don't see it," I replied.

"Trust me," whispered Alexia. "She's pregnant. My mom looked like that when she was pregnant."

"Shhhhh!" whispered Andrea. "It's none of your business whether or not Ms.

Greene is pregnant. That's personal."

I guess Ms. Greene heard us whispering, because she said, "Yes, I'm pregnant! This is a teachable moment!"

Ugh, I hate teachable moments. It means we have to learn stuff.

"Who knows what circumference is?" asked Ms. Greene.

Sir Cumference? Was he one of the knights of the round table?

"Not me."

"Not me."

"Not me."

In case you were wondering, nobody knew what circumference was. But then, of course, Andrea stuck her hand in the air and waved it around like she was washing a big window. Ms. Greene called on her.

"Circumference is the distance around a circle," Andrea said.

"That's right!"

Andrea smiled the smile she smiles to let everybody know she knows something nobody else knows. Ms. Greene took a tape measure out of her purse.

"Let's measure the circumference of my tummy!" she said excitedly.

We all gathered around Ms. Greene and wrapped the tape measure around her tummy. It came out to thirty-six inches, or about ninety-one centimeters.

Ms. Greene told us there are twelve

inches in a foot and three feet in a yard.
Twelve times three is thirty-six. So the circumference of Ms. Greene's tummy is one
yard.

"A football field is a hundred yards,"
said Michael. "So you could roll down a
football field a hundred times."

"That's right!" said Ms. Greene, "but I

don't think I'm going to do that."

"Can we measure your tummy *every* Monday?" asked Emily. "That way we can see if the circumference of your tummy changes."

"Sure!" said Ms. Greene.

Emily should get the Nobel Prize for that idea. That's a prize they give out to people who don't have bells.

Ms. Greene was about to put the tape measure away, but then she stopped and snapped her fingers. Grown-ups always snap their fingers when they have an idea. Nobody knows why.

She went out in the hallway for a minute. When she came back, she had our science teacher, Mr. Docker, with her.

"Let's measure some teachers!" Ms. Greene said excitedly.

"Is Mr. Docker pregnant?" I asked.

"Not that I know of," said Mr. Docker. Everybody laughed.

"No," said Ms. Greene. "Let's see how *tall* Mr. Docker is."

We stood Mr. Docker against the wall and measured him. He was sixty inches tall. Then we stood Miss Banks against the wall and measured her. She was seventy inches tall. Then we stood Ms. Greene against the wall and measured her. She was sixty-five inches tall.*

---

*Parallel lines have so much in common. Too bad they'll never meet.

"Do you know how to calculate our average height?" asked Ms. Greene.

"No," said Ryan.

"Nope," said Alexia.

"No clue," said Michael.

Even Little Miss Know-It-All didn't know the answer.

"It's simple," said Ms. Greene. "We just add up all three numbers and divide the total by the number of people."

She went to the whiteboard and added seventy plus sixty plus sixty-five. That came to a hundred ninety-five. Then she divided a hundred ninety-five by three. That came to sixty-five.

"So the average height of all three of you is sixty-five inches," said Andrea. "That means you are exactly the average, Ms. Greene."

"That's right," she replied. "And another way of saying the word 'average' is to use the word 'mean.' Our mean height is sixty-five inches."

"Ms. Greene is mean," I said.

Hey, that would make a good book title!

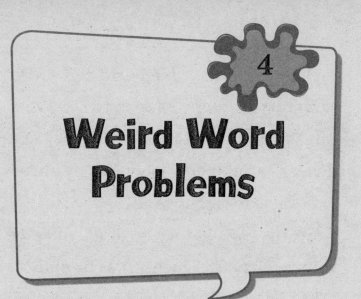

Weird Word Problems

The first thing we did the next Monday was to measure Ms. Greene's circumference. We got out the tape measure and wrapped it around her. She was now thirty-seven inches, or about ninety-four centimeters.

"Your circumference is one inch bigger," said Neil.

"Okay," said Ms. Greene. "It's time to turn on our math brains."

She put her fingers on her ear lobes and pretended to turn them while making clicking noises. We all put our fingers on our ear lobes and pretended to turn them while making clicking noises.

"Good," said Ms. Greene. "Today we're going to work on word problems."

NOOOOOOO!

Not word problems! *Anything* but word problems!* I hate word problems. Math is supposed to be about numbers, not words. This was the worst thing to happen since National Poetry Month.

---

*Why are equal signs so modest? Because they know they're not greater than or less than anybody else.

29

"Everybody, stand up on your chair," said Ms. Greene.

Huh? That made no sense at all. But we all got up on our chairs, because when grown-ups tell us to do stuff, we do it. And besides, standing on a chair is fun.

"Repeat after me," said Ms. Greene. "I AM A PROBLEM-SOLVING MACHINE!"

"I AM A PROBLEM-SOLVING MA-CHINE!" we all shouted.

"I AM NOT AFRAID OF YOU!" said Ms. Greene.

"I AM NOT AFRAID OF YOU!" we all shouted.

"YOU'RE JUST A WORD PROBLEM!" said Ms. Greene.

"YOU'RE JUST A WORD PROBLEM!" we all shouted.

"YOU DON'T SCARE ME!" said Ms. Greene.

"YOU DON'T SCARE ME!" we all shouted.

"Okay, everybody, sit down," said Ms. Greene. "Here's a word problem. Sixteen polka-dotted elephants escaped from Michael's house . . ."

"What?" said Michael.

"And fourteen flying monkeys escaped from Ryan's house . . ."

"WHAT?" said Ryan.

"And twenty *T. rex* dinosaurs escaped from Alexia's house . . ."

"WHAT?" said Alexia.

"And all the animals decided to have a party at Neil's house . . ."

"Why *my* house?" asked Neil.

"But half of them got lost on the way over," said Ms. Greene. "How many animals showed up at Neil's house?"

That was a weird word problem. We all got out pencils and paper to figure out how many animals showed up at Neil's house. I added sixteen plus fourteen plus twenty to get fifty animals altogether. And if half of them got lost, the answer is . . .

"Fifty!" shouted Emily.

"Fifty-four!" shouted Neil.

"Thirty-five!" shouted Michael.

"Twenty-five!" Andrea and I shouted at the same time.

"That's right!" said Ms. Greene. "Very good!"

"I got the answer first," said Andrea. "You just copied me."

"I did not," I told her. "*I* got the answer first."

"Ooooh!" said Ryan. "A.J. and Andrea shouted out the answer at the same time. They must be in LOVE!"

"When are you gonna get married?" asked Michael.

If those guys weren't my friends, I would hate them.

Ms. Greene said the best way to practice word problems is to make some up yourself. So each of us had five minutes to think of a word problem. She said to try and make it personal, so everybody in the class would be able to picture it in our heads.

We started writing out word problems. I didn't know what to write. I pretended that my pencil was a rocket ship.

"Three minutes left," said Ms. Greene.

One by one, everybody finished writing

their word problem. I couldn't think of anything. I was concentrating so hard that my brain hurt.

"Two minutes left," said Ms. Greene.

My mind was blank. I hate when that happens! I just couldn't think of a good word problem.

"Pencils down," said Ms. Greene. "Okay, let's hear your word problems. Andrea?"

Andrea read a word problem about thousands of monarch butterflies traveling from Canada to Mexico. She showed how to subtract the ones that died from the total to calculate how many survived. It was easy to do because I could picture the butterflies in my head.

Ryan read his word problem about an army of pickles that started a war against an army of cucumbers. That was weird, but I figured out the answer because I could picture the pickles and cucumbers in my head.

Well, I didn't have pickles and cucumbers in my head. You know what I mean.

Alexia read her word problem about a cowboy who was trying to round up a herd of sheep but some of them just wanted to dance around with Hula-Hoops. That was weird, too, but I could picture the sheep Hula-Hooping in my head.

Everybody presented a weird word problem. Everybody but me.

"How about you, A.J.?" asked Ms. Greene. "What did you come up with?"

I wanted to go to Antarctica and live with the penguins. Penguins don't have to make up word problems. I didn't know what to do. I didn't know what to say. I had to think fast.

"Okay, there were these sharks," I said.

"How many sharks?" asked Neil.

"A hundred," I said. "And they were attacking people on the beach."

"I'm scared," said Emily.

"How many people were on the beach?" asked Ryan.

"A million hundred," I told him. "And they were running away from the sharks."

"A million hundred isn't a real number," said Andrea, who thinks she knows everything.

"Go on, A.J.," said Ms. Greene.

I didn't know what to say next. I was just making it up as I went along.

"So the sharks go to the zoo," I continued.

"How would sharks get to a zoo?" asked Michael.

"They took an Uber," I replied.

"Why did they go to the zoo?" asked Michael.

"To free the other animals," I explained. "So the lions and tigers and elephants all ran out the front gate of the zoo."

"Go on," said Ms. Greene.

"And there was a giant catapult there," I said.

"Why was there a giant catapult?" asked Emily.

"There just *was*, okay?" I told her.

"Is there a word problem in here, A.J.?" asked Ms. Greene.

"Yeah," I said. "The question is, how many flying elephants landed on Andrea's head?"

It was ridorkulous, but everybody laughed, because they could all picture a bunch of elephants flying off a catapult and landing on Andrea's head.

"That's not nice, Arlo!" said Andrea, who calls me by my real name because she knows I don't like it. "I don't approve of violence."

"What do you have against violins?" I asked.

"Not violins! Violence!" shouted Andrea.

I know the difference between violins and violence. I was just yanking Andrea's chain. She needs to get a sense of humor transplant. My word problem was great.

5

Mathmagic

The next Monday, we measured the circumference of Ms. Greene's belly like we did every week. It was 38 inches around, or about 96.5 centimeters.

"She's getting bigger," said Neil.

Ms. Greene said she had to step out of the room for a minute. When she came back, she looked completely different. She was wearing a black cape and a top hat. That was weird.

"I thought you were a mathematician," said Andrea.

"Today I'm a math*magician*!" Ms. Greene said as she pulled out a magic wand. "We're going to do some math-*magic*!"

I never heard of mathmagic. I bet she made up that word. But Ms. Greene said she was going to show us some math tricks.*

"Who can tell me what seven times seven is?" she asked.

Andrea shot her hand in the air first, of course.

"Seven times seven equals forty-nine," she said proudly.

"That's right," said Ms. Greene. "And how do you know that?"

"I just memorized it," said Andrea.

"Well, here's a little trick to help everybody remember," said Ms. Greene. "Think of the San Francisco 49ers. Seven

---

*Math class is so long because the teacher keeps going off on tangents.

touchdowns with extra points add up to forty-nine."

"I love the 49ers!" said Michael.

"How about six times seven?" asked Ms. Greene. "What does that equal?"

"Forty-two!" shouted Andrea.

"Right!" said Ms. Greene. "Just remember this—six and seven went on a date for two. For two. Forty-two! So six times seven equals forty-two."

"That's a cool trick," said Ryan.

"How about seven times eight?" asked Ms. Greene.

"Fifty-six!" shouted Andrea.

"Yes," said Ms. Greene. "Before you go to the seventh and eighth grades, you have to go to the fifth and sixth grades. Five, six, seven, eight. So you get fifty-six when you multiply seven times eight."

"It's like magic!" said Alexia.

Ms. Greene knows all kinds of math tricks like that.

"King Henry died drinking chocolate milk!" she said. Then she explained that's how you remember the order of the metric system—kilo, hecto, deca, deci, centi, and milli.

"Hairy toes only!" said Ms. Greene. Then she explained that's how you remember hundreds, tens, and ones.

"Dirty monkeys smell bad!" said Ms. Greene. Then she explained that's how you remember the four basic steps of long division—divide, multiply, subtract,

and bring down. She drew this on the
board . . .

$$2\overline{)76}$$

Ms. Greene showed us that first you
DIVIDE the seven by two, which is three
with one left over. Then you MULTIPLY
three times two, which is six. Then you
SUBTRACT six from seven, which is one.
Then you BRING DOWN the next number, which is six. Then you divide again,

two into sixteen. That's eight. So seventy-six divided by two equals thirty-eight.

"See?" said Ms. Greene. "Divide, multiply, subtract, and bring down. Just say 'dirty monkeys smell bad!'"

"You could also say 'dad, mom, sister, brother,'" said Neil.

"Or you could say 'Does McDonald's sell burgers,'" said Alexia.

"Or 'Dracula must suck blood'!" I said.

"Whatever trick works for you," said Ms. Greene. "If you remember those words, you'll remember the steps of long division. Any questions?"

"If you're a mathmagician," I said, "can you saw Andrea in half?" Everybody laughed except Andrea. She made a mean face.

"Half of anything is fifty percent of it," said Ms. Greene. "Divide anything by two and you get half of it. Two halves make a whole. Halftime is the middle of a game. Half of a half is a quarter *blah blah blah blah* . . .

She went on and on like that. While she was talking, Andrea put her hand in the air. Of *course*.

"Ms. Greene," she said, "I don't understand improper fractions. Can you explain them?"

Improper fractions? I never even *heard* of improper fractions. Andrea must have read ahead in our math book. What is her problem?

"Sure," said Ms. Greene. "Everybody, stand up."

We all stood up.

"An improper fraction has a numerator that's bigger than its denominator," she said. "So imagine for a moment that your head is a numerator, and your butt is a denominator."

We all laughed because Ms. Greene said "butt." It's okay to say "but" in school, but we're not supposed to add a T to it. Nobody knows why.

"Is your head bigger than your butt?"

asked Ms. Greene. "No! It wouldn't be proper to have a head bigger than your butt. So a fraction with a numerator bigger than its denominator is an improper fraction."

That made sense, I guess.

"Everybody, shake your numerator!" shouted Ms. Greene.

We all shook our heads.

"Okay, now shake your denominator!" shouted Ms. Greene.

We all shook our butts. Then Ms. Greene told us to sit on our denominators.

A Surprise Guest

6

The next Monday, we measured Ms. Greene's circumference, and it was thirty-nine inches, or about ninety-nine centimeters.

"She's getting bigger," said Neil.

"Are you ready for NUMMM-BERS?" Ms. Greene shouted. "We have a special guest today. . . ."

That's when the weirdest thing in the history of the world happened. The sound of drums and bass started pounding out of a boom box in the hallway. Purple smoke started pouring out on the floor. Laser beams started shooting around the room.

"ARE YOU READY TO GET DOWN?" Ms. Greene hollered over the music. "ARE YOU READY TO LEARN SOME MATH?"*

"Yeah!" we all screamed.

"Now," she shouted, "appearing live at Ella Mentry School . . . is the one . . . the only . . . Jam Master Hynde, the One-Man Funky Groove Machine!"

-----

*I had an argument with a ninety-degree angle. It turned out to be right.

And you'll never believe who came boogeying into the room. It was Mr. Hynde, our old music teacher! He left our school after he appeared on *American Idol* and became a famous rapper. You can read about him in a book called *Mr. Hynde Is Out of His Mind!*

Mr. Hynde was wearing a backward baseball cap and a purple cape with sequins all over it. He had on sunglasses, too, even though we were indoors.

"Gimme a beat!" shouted Mr. Hynde.

Ryan, Michael, and I started beatboxing. The drums got louder. The lights got brighter. And then Mr. Hynde started rapping. . . .

I'm not gonna lie
to you girls and guys.
Don't be shy.
No need to cry.
I'll tell you why.
It's time for us to mul-ti-ply!

Mr. Hynde threw off his purple cape and started break dancing. Then he spun around on his head and kept rapping . . .

Two times one is two,
you know what to do.
Two times two is four,
wanna hear some more?
Two times three is six,

add that to the mix.

Two times four is eight,

I give it to you straight.

Two times five is ten,

I won't say it again.

Two times six is twelve,

say it to yourselves.

Two times seven is fourteen,

put it on the big screen.

Two times eight is sixteen,

soon this will be routine.

Two times nine is eighteen,

I think I need more caffeine.

Two times ten is twenty,

and I say that is plenty!

"Can you rap about the eight times table?" shouted Ms. Greene. "Kids often have trouble with that one."

Mr. Hynde didn't miss a beat. He started freestyling . . .

I ate and ate 'til I puked on the floor,
so eight times eight is sixty-four!

Everybody laughed because Mr. Hynde said "puked."

Six and eight went on a date,
and they came home before eight.
Before eight. B-four-eight.
So six times eight is forty-eight!

"How about rounding numbers?" shouted Ms. Greene.

Mr. Hynde didn't even need to stop and think. He just freestyled again . . .

I round numbers all the time.
All you need's a little rhyme . . .
Five and above, give it a shove,
Four and below, keep it low!

"How about multiple-digit subtraction when you need to borrow from the next column?" shouted Ms. Greene.

Huh?

Mr. Hynde stopped for a moment. It looked like he didn't know what to say.

Maybe he didn't even know what multiple-digit subtraction is. So Ms. Greene wrote this problem on the board . . .

$$
\begin{array}{r}
2{,}056 \\
-\ 1{,}027 \\
\hline
1{,}029
\end{array}
$$

Mr. Hynde looked at the board. Then he smiled and started freestyling again . . .

If you gotta buncha digits
you need to subtract,
this is what you do
to get it exact.
If there's more on the floor,
go next door

$$\begin{array}{r} 2,056 \\ -1,027 \\ \hline 1,029 \end{array}$$

and get one more.
If there's more on the top,
no need to stop.
If both numbers are the same,
zero's the game!

Everybody clapped, cheered, and gave
Mr. Hynde a standing ovation. You should

have been there! We got to see it live and in person. Then we formed a conga line and started dancing around the room. It was hilarious.

If there's more on the floor,
go next door
and get one more.
If there's more on the top,
no need to stop.
If both numbers are the same,
zero's the game!

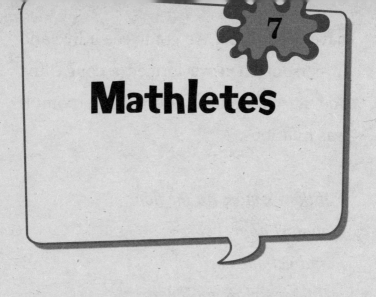

Mathletes

The next Monday, we measured Ms. Greene's circumference. It was 40 inches, or about 102 centimeters.

"She's getting bigger," said Neil.

"Are you ready for NUMMM-BERS?" shouted Ms. Greene. "Follow me!"

She led us out of the classroom and

down the hall. Then we made a left at the corner. Then we made a right.

"Where is she taking us?" Alexia asked.

"Beats me," I replied.

We walked a million hundred miles until we were standing outside the gym. That's where we have Fizz Ed—my favorite subject. I love Fizz Ed because we don't have to learn stuff. We can just play games and have fun.

Our Fizz Ed teacher, Miss Small, opened the door. She is really tall, so her name makes no sense at all. One time, she fell out of a tree and broke her leg. You can read about it in a book called *Miss Small Is off the Wall!*

"Wait a minute," said Andrea. "We don't have Fizz Ed on Mondays."

"That's right," said Miss Small. "You're not athletes today. You're *mathletes*!"

Uh-oh. Something told me we were going to have to learn stuff. Not fair! We

went into the gym. Ms. Greene sat on the bleachers while Miss Small told us to do jumping jacks.

"What does this have to do with math?" asked Andrea.

"Two . . . four . . . six . . . eight . . . ten . . ." chanted Miss Small as we did jumping jacks.

"That's called skip counting," shouted Ms. Greene.

"Three . . . six . . . nine . . . twelve . . . fifteen . . ." chanted Miss Small.

"It helps you learn your multiplication tables," shouted Ms. Greene.

"Four . . . eight . . . twelve . . . sixteen . . . twenty . . ." chanted Miss Small. "Five . . .

ten . . . fifteen . . . twenty . . ."

We did a million hundred jumping jacks. By the time we got up to the six times table, I thought I was gonna die. We were all panting, which means we were wearing pants.

"Math is *exhausting*," said Neil.*

After that, Miss Small had us stand in a circle and throw a ball back and forth while we skip counted some more.

"Ten . . . twenty . . . thirty . . . forty . . . fifty," she chanted. "Okay, it's time for Nerf Blaster Math!"

HUH? That's also "HUH" spelled backward.

---

*Want to make seven an even number? Just remove the S.

Miss Small had set up a bunch of targets, and each one had an addition, subtraction, multiplication, or division problem on it. There were a bunch of other targets off to the side that had numbers on them.

"First, knock down a math problem," said Miss Small. "Then knock down the correct answer to the problem."

She said I could go first. I picked up a Nerf Blaster and aimed it at the easiest target—it read "2 + 2." I pulled the trigger, but I missed. I hit the target that read "8 × 8." Oh, *man*! I don't know what eight times eight equals!

"Can I try again?" I asked.

"NO!" everybody shouted.

"Figure it out, Arlo!" said Andrea.

I didn't know what to say. I didn't know what to do. I had to think fast. And then I remembered . . .

I ate and ate 'til I puked on the floor,
So eight times eight is sixty-four!

"Sixty-four!" I shouted.

"Very good, A.J.!" shouted Ms. Greene.

I stuck my tongue out at Andrea. I aimed the Nerf Blaster at the target with the number sixty-four on it and knocked it down. We all took turns hitting the targets.

"Nice job!" shouted Miss Small. "Now it's time for Subtraction Bowling!"

Huh?

Miss Small led us to a little bowling alley she had set up on the other side of the gym. At the end of the alley were ten cardboard paper towel rolls standing up like bowling pins. She gave Michael a ball and told him to roll it down the alley and see how many pins he could knock down.

Michael rolled the ball and knocked down seven pins.

"How many are left?" asked Miss Small.

"Three!" we all shouted.

"Correct!" said Miss Small. "When you subtract seven from ten, you have three left."

She gave Michael another ball to take a second shot. He knocked down one of the three pins.

"How many are left?" Miss Small asked.

"Two!" we all shouted.

"Correct!"

Miss Small set up all the pins again and handed Alexia a ball. She knocked down four pins.

"How many are left?" Miss Small asked.

"Six!" we all shouted.

Each of us got two turns except for Andrea, who knocked down all ten pins in her first try. Of *course*.

"How many are left?"

"Zero!" we all shouted.

Subtraction Bowling is fun. We played a bunch of other math games. Then the bell rang, and we had to go back to class and learn stuff again. Bummer in the summer! I wish we had Fizz Ed all day long.

Eating Our Schoolwork

The next Monday, we measured Ms. Greene's circumference, and it was 41 inches, or about 104 centimeters.

"She's getting bigger," said Neil.

"We have a special guest today," announced Ms. Greene.

Not *another* one!

"Follow me!"

We walked a million hundred miles until we were standing outside the vomitorium. It used to be called the cafetorium until some kid threw up in there.

"What are we doing *here*?" asked Alexia. "It's not lunchtime."

Our lunch lady, Ms. Hall, opened the door and greeted us. She's weird. One time, she made cupcakes out of meatballs and mashed potatoes. She also roller-skates while juggling veggies. You can read about her in a book called *Ms. Hall Is a Goofball!*

"I have a special surprise for you this morning," said Ms. Hall. "We're going to

make a pancake, and then we're going to eat it!"

"Just *one* pancake?" I asked.

"Yup," said Ms. Hall. "Just one."

That didn't sound like a very good idea to me. There were seven of us. I could eat three or four pancakes all by myself. One pancake wasn't going to be enough.

"This is called the batter," Ms. Hall said as she mixed some eggs, flour, milk, butter, and sugar in a bowl.

Hey, why do they call that stuff batter? Pancakes have nothing to do with baseball.

Anyway, Ms. Hall had us whip the batter with this thing called a whisk. Too bad she didn't have a knoof.

Next, she poured the batter into a giant pan that had been heating up on the stove. The batter spread all the way across the pan. That's when I realized why she was only making one pancake. It was going to be a *really big* pancake.

"This will be the biggest pancake in the

history of the world," said Ryan.

Soon the pancake was sizzling. It smelled really good. I love pancakes. A pancake is like a cake in a pan, so it has the perfect name.

"What does this have to do with math?" asked Andrea.*

---

*I don't trust my math teacher. I saw her holding a piece of graph paper. She must be plotting something.

"Oh, pancakes are *all* about math!" said Ms. Greene. "Today we're going to learn more about fractions. Can anybody tell me the definition of the word 'fraction'?"

"I can!" I said.

"You can not, Arlo," Andrea told me.

"Oh, yeah?" I said. "To show you how good I am at fractions, last night I only did *half* my homework."

You may think that was a joke, but it wasn't. Here's a joke about fractions . . .

Do you know which king loved fractions? Henry the Eighth.

Get it?

Anyway, Ms. Hall flipped the giant pancake over. Then she said it was finished cooking and we could eat it. I could have eaten the whole thing myself, but Ms. Hall said we'd have to divide it up evenly so it would be fair to everybody. She got out a big knife. Too bad she didn't have a knoof.

"Let's see, there are seven of you kids, plus me," said Ms. Hall, "so we should cut the pancake into eight pieces."

"What about Ms. Greene?" asked Emily.

"No thanks," said Ms. Greene. "I'm like the two fours that skipped lunch."

"HUH?"

"I already ate," said Ms. Greene. "Get it? Two fours? I already ate? Already eight?"

I think Ms. Greene has been hanging around Mrs. Stoker too much.

Ms. Hall started cutting the giant pancake.

"Andrea," she said, "would you like one-fourth of the pancake, or one-eighth of the pancake?"

"I would like one-fourth, please," said Andrea.

"How about you, A.J.?" Ms. Hall said. Would you like one-fourth or one-eighth of the pancake?"

"I want one-eighth," I said. "Eight is bigger than four, so I'll get the bigger piece."

See, that's why I'm in the gifted and talented program. I know my math. I stuck my tongue out at Andrea. Nah-nah-nah boo-boo on her.

Ms. Hall gave Andrea and I each a piece of the pancake on paper plates. The only problem was that Andrea's piece was way bigger than mine!

"Actually," said Ms. Hall, "one-fourth is *twice* as big as one-eighth. You see, as the numbers in the denominator get larger, you're dividing the pancake into smaller and smaller pieces."

Not fair! Andrea stuck her tongue out at me. Why can't a truck full of giant pancakes fall on her head?

"There are eight pieces of pancake," said Ms. Hall. "So each piece is one-eighth of the whole pancake."

"So eight-eighths would be the whole pancake," said Little Miss Know-It-All.

"Right," said Ms. Greene. "How many eighths of the pancake is half of it?"

"Four-eighths would be half," said Neil, "because four is half of eight."

"That's right," said Ms. Greene. "And what happens if you split each half in half?"

Nobody raised their hand.

"That would be two-eighths," said Ms. Greene. "Two-eighths is the same as one-fourth or a quarter of the pancake or twenty-five percent of the pancake *blah blah blah blah . . .*"

She went on like that for a million hundred minutes. I think it had something to do with fractions.

Finally, Ms. Hall gave a piece of the

pancake to everybody. Then she gave us maple syrup to drizzle on top. We finished eating the whole thing in a few seconds. Yum!

"We're eating our schoolwork!" Michael said as he licked his plate clean.

That's when the weirdest thing in the history of the world happened. Somebody came running into the vomitorium.

Well, that's not the weird part. People come running into the vomitorium all the time. The weird part was *who* came running into the vomitorium. It was our after-school program director, Mr. Tony!

He's always trying to set world records so he can get into the Guinness World Records. You can read about him in *Mr.*

Tony Is Full of Baloney! But we hardly ever see him during school hours.

"I heard you made the biggest pancake in the world," Mr. Tony shouted.

"We did!" said Ms. Hall.

"It was ginormous!" I told Mr. Tony.

"Can I see it?" he asked. "The biggest pancake in the world would be a great way to get into the Guinness World Records."

"We ate it," we all said.

"NOOOOOOOOOOOOOO!"

A Big Problem

The next Monday, Ms. Greene's circumference was 42 inches, or about 107 centimeters.

"She's getting bigger!" said Neil.

"Today we have a special guest," said Ms. Greene.

Not *again*! You'll never believe who

walked into the door at that moment.

Nobody! People don't walk into doors, at least not on purpose. Didn't we go over that in Chapter One? But you'll never believe who walked into the door*way*.

It was Miss Daisy, our teacher when we were in second grade! You can read about her in a book called *Miss Daisy Is Crazy!*

Now Miss Daisy is called "Mrs. Daisy." That's because she got married to our reading specialist, Mr. Macky. Then she stopped teaching when she had a baby. Every so often, she comes back to school as a substitute. You can read about *that* in a book called *Miss Daisy Is STILL Crazy!*

Ms. Greene told us she lives on the same street as Mrs. Daisy. They gave each other a big hug. Grown-ups are always hugging each other. Nobody knows why.

"I invited Mrs. Daisy to help us with math," said Ms. Greene.

No way! When Mrs. Daisy was our teacher, she didn't even know how to multiply four times four. She doesn't know *anything* about math.*

"Actually," said Mrs. Daisy, "I have a problem I'm hoping you kids can help me with."

"What's the matter?" asked Ms. Greene.

"I have a vegetable garden in my back-yard," said Mrs. Daisy, "and bunnies are eating my veggies."

"That *is* a problem," replied Ms. Greene.

"What does that have to do with math?" asked Andrea.

"Oh, nothing," said Mrs. Daisy. "It just bothers me that bunnies are eating my veggies."

---

*Did you hear about the mathematician who was afraid of negative numbers? He'll stop at nothing to avoid them.

"Why don't you put a fence around your garden?" suggested Ryan.

"That's a good idea," said Mrs. Daisy. "I never thought of that."

She never thinks of *anything*. We told Mrs. Daisy that she could go to Home Depot and buy some wire fencing to keep the bunnies out of her garden.

"Gee, I never bought fencing before," she said. "How do you buy a fence?"

"They sell it by the foot," said Michael.

Mrs. Daisy looked confused. She looked at her shoes.

"I don't want to buy a foot," she said. "I want to buy a fence."

"No, a foot is twelve inches long,"

explained Neil. "You can buy as many feet of fencing as you need."

Duh! Everybody knows that. Everybody except Mrs. Daisy. We asked her how big her garden was, but of course she didn't know. She doesn't know anything.

"I've seen your garden," said Ms. Greene. "It's about twenty feet long and ten feet wide."

"But how will I know how much fencing to buy?" asked Mrs. Daisy.

It was simple. I didn't even need to use a pencil and paper. If her garden is twenty feet long and ten feet wide, she'll need two pieces of fence that are twenty feet long and two pieces of fence that are ten feet long. Twenty plus twenty equals forty, and ten plus ten equals twenty. Forty plus twenty equals sixty. So Mrs. Daisy needs to buy sixty feet of fencing to keep the bunnies out of her garden.

We tried to explain that to her, but her forehead got all wrinkly like an accordion. When a grown-up gets wrinkly accordion face, it means they're confused.

"I don't understand," said Mrs. Daisy.

Oh, man! Ryan and I got out of our seats and drew a rectangle on the whiteboard. I wrote the word "Garden" in the middle of it, so Mrs. Daisy would know what I was talking about. Ryan labeled the four sides of the garden with "20," "10," "20," and "10."

"All you have to do is add the numbers together," I explained.

"Twenty ... thirty ... fifty ... sixty," said Ryan. "So you need sixty feet of fencing to keep the bunnies out of your garden."

Mrs. Daisy still had wrinkly accordion face.

"I just don't get it," she said.

I slapped my forehead. How did Mrs. Daisy ever become a teacher? We explained everything again, but she *still* didn't get it.

Ms. Greene told Mrs. Daisy that she would go to Home Depot with her and help buy the fencing she needs. That's when the weirdest thing in the history of the world happened.

But I'm not going to tell you what it was.

Okay, okay, I'll tell you. But you have to read the next chapter.

Multiplication

After we figured out how much fencing Mrs. Daisy needed for her garden, Mrs. Stoker walked into the room.

"I just wanted to see how you kids were making out," she said.

"Ugh! Gross! Disgusting!" we shouted.

"Do you want to hear some math jokes?" asked Mrs. Stoker.

"Yes!" shouted all the girls.

"No!" shouted all the boys.

"What did the acorn say when he grew up?" asked Mrs. Stoker.

"What?" we all shouted.

"Geometry!" said Mrs. Stoker. "Get it? Gee, I'm a tree?"

Okay, that was almost funny.

"Who's the king of the pencil case?" asked Mrs. Stoker.

"Who?"

"The ruler!" shouted Mrs. Stoker. "But seriously, why did the mathematician spill his food in the oven?"

"Why?"

"The recipe said to put it in the oven at a

hundred eighty degrees! Get it? Degrees?"

We pretended to laugh at Mrs. Stoker's jokes even though they weren't very funny.

"How about this one?" said Mrs. Stoker. "If I had six oranges in one hand and four apples in the other hand, what would I have?"

"Really big hands!" I shouted.

"That's right!" Mrs. Stoker said. "I got a million of 'em. Did you hear about the math teacher who—"

But she didn't get the chance to finish her sentence.

"I think it's time," Ms. Greene suddenly said.

"Time to teach us to add and subtract fractions?" Andrea asked.

"No," said Ms. Greene.

"Time for us to learn decimals?" asked Andrea.

"No," Ms. Greene said a little louder.

"Time to teach us quadrilaterals?" asked Andrea.

"No!" shouted Ms. Greene. "It's time for me to go to the hospital! I'm going to have the babies!"

WHAT?! I looked at Ryan. Ryan looked at Emily. Emily looked at Andrea. Andrea looked at Neil. We were all looking at each other.

"Did you say *babies*?" asked Neil.

"Yes!" shouted Ms. Greene.

"Do you mean you're having more than one baby?" asked Andrea.

"YES!"

"You're having twins?" asked Emily.

"Keep going," said Ms. Greene.

"Triplets?" said Neil. "You're going to have *three* babies?"

"No!" shouted Ms. Greene as she held her tummy. "I'm having quadruplets!"

"Quad means four!" shouted Andrea. "That's four babies!"

WHAT?!

"MS. GREENE IS MULTIPLYING!" I shouted.

"Well," said Andrea, "you *could* say that

she's adding one plus one plus one plus one."

"No, she's multiplying," I said. "One times four equals four."

"She's *adding*," insisted Andrea.

"She's multiplying!" I shouted.

"Oooh!" said Ryan. "A.J. and Andrea are arguing about math. They must be in LOVE!"

"When are you gonna get married?" asked Michael.

"Who *cares* whether she's adding or multiplying?" shouted Mrs. Daisy. "We've got to get her to the hospital!"

"Can you drive her, Mrs. Daisy?" asked Alexia.

"I don't know how to drive," said Mrs. Daisy, who doesn't know how to do anything.

"Can you drive her, Mrs. Stoker?" asked Emily.

"I walked to school today," Mrs. Stoker replied.

"Get another teacher!" shouted Neil. "Quick!"

"No time for that!" shouted Alexia. "We need to call an ambulance!"

"Hurry!" yelled Ms. Greene.

"Somebody, get her purse!" shouted Emily.

"Get her coat!" shouted Andrea.

Everybody was running around, yelling

and screaming and bumping into each other.

"Run for your lives!" shouted Neil.

Finally, our school nurse, Mrs. Cooney, came rushing into the room. She led Ms. Greene away and drove her to the hospital.

Ms. Greene had four healthy babies. They were all boys. She named them George (for "geometry"), Alan (for "algebra"), Calvin (for "calculus"), and Trig (for "trigonometry," whatever *that* is).

Man, Ms. Greene *really* loves math.*

---

*If you want to keep warm in a cold room, go to the corner. It's ninety degrees.

Well, that's pretty much what happened. After it was over, we went to visit Ms. Greene in the hospital. The babies were really cute.

I was thinking . . . if Ms. Greene had four babies and if each of them farts twenty times a day . . . That would be 80 farts a day, 560 farts a week, 29,120 farts a year. That's a lot of farts!

It only goes to prove my point—math stinks!

Maybe our math scores will improve. Maybe Mrs. Daisy will buy enough fencing to stop the bunnies from eating the veggies in her garden. Maybe we'll find out who Sir Cumference was. Maybe Ms. Greene will roll down a football field. Maybe I'll puke on the floor. Maybe a bunch of polka-dotted elephants will escape from Michael's house. Maybe King Henry really *did* die drinking chocolate milk. Maybe my head is full of pickles and cucumbers. Maybe somebody will invent a knoof.

But it won't be easy!

More weird books from Dan Gutman

My Weird School

My Weird School Graphic Novels

My Weirder School

My Weirdest School

 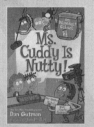

My Weirder-est School

My Weirdtastic School

My Weird School Fast Facts

My Weird School Daze

HARPER
An Imprint of HarperCollinsPublishers

harpercollinschildrens.com